Ella

The Duchess
Who Became a Saint

by Maria Tobias

Conciliar Press
Ben Lomond, California

ELLA'S STORY:
The Duchess Who Became a Saint

Text © Copyright 2004 by Maria Tobias
Illustrations © Copyright 2004 by Bonnie Gillis

Published by   Conciliar Press
                    P.O. Box 76
                    Ben Lomond, California 95005-0076

Printed in the United States of America

ISBN 1-888212-70-5

Manufactured under the direction of Double Eagle Industries.
For manufacturing details, call 888-824-4344
or e-mail to info@publishingquest.com

I dedicate this book to my daughter, Elizabeth.
I hope that she finds the life of her patron saint,
Elizabeth the New Martyr,
an inspiration for her own life.

Chapter One

Ella sat down with a sigh on the chair in her bedroom. She rubbed her sore feet and tried to pin back her long, blonde hair. Normally she felt a sense of peace in this room that she shared with her sister, Victoria, but not today. She was almost too tired to feel anything.

"Why does Mama always make us help her care for others," she thought with resentment. "Why do we have to work so hard when it's almost Christmas!"

She thought back over her tiring day. Even though it was December twenty-third, Ella and her sisters and brother had not spent the day at parties or having fun. Instead, she and her sister Victoria had served food at a dinner arranged by their mother. It wasn't an ordinary

Christmas dinner attended by cheerful neighbors in colorful holiday clothes. No friends arrived with mysterious presents in bright, crackling paper. Instead, the dinner was given for the children of the servants in Ella's house.

"Ninety-one children!" thought Ella as she looked down at her hands, red from the hot plates she had rushed to the table all evening. "I don't see why we had to give them a party. It's not like anyone else we know gives parties for their servants."

A few weeks ago, Ella's mother, Princess Alice, had announced to her two eldest daughters that they would need to help her with the celebration she was planning for the servant children. They were to help set the dinner table and serve mince pie and roast goose.

"The poor things almost never get a treat," she had said, looking seriously at her daughters. "I know you two will want the children to have this special Christmas dinner."

Ella and Victoria had agreed to help, even though they

would rather have played dress-up with their mother's clothes. The girls loved to burrow into Princess Alice's closet to choose old silk dresses and shawls for their games of make-believe. Often they would act out fairy tales such as Cinderella or Sleeping Beauty. Suddenly, Ella's thoughts were interrupted by a soft knock at her door.

"Elizabeth?" she heard her mother's voice call.

"Yes, Mama, I'm here," responded Ella.

Her mother only called her Elizabeth when she had something serious to say. Ella quickly stood up and straightened her dress. Even though her mother, Princess Alice, was kind, she did not tolerate her children being untidy.

Princess Alice entered the bedroom and sat down on a small armchair in the corner of the room. Grouped around the worn but comfortable seat was Ella's and Victoria's childhood collection of china dolls.

"Elizabeth, dear," Princess Alice said, looking seriously into her daughter's eyes. "Why did you leave the dinner early? We hadn't finished giving the presents to the children. Everyone wondered where you went."

Elizabeth blushed. It was true that she had slipped out of the dining hall early. She had wanted to walk in the garden and visit her pet animals before bedtime. She and her sisters and brother kept a whole "Noah's Ark" of animals, as her father sometimes joked. Ella loved their tame fox best, while Victoria preferred the sheep and rabbits.

"I'm sorry, Mama," answered Ella, embarrassed, "I wanted to visit the animals before bedtime. My little fox was getting hungry."

Instead of scolding her, Princess Alice looked down

quietly at her hands for a minute or so. Then she looked up at Ella.

"Ella, did I ever tell you the story of your name?" she asked.

"Well, I know I was named after our ancestor, Saint Elizabeth of Hungary," answered Ella in a puzzled voice. Why was her mother using this moment to discuss the history of her name?

"Yes, that's true," said Princess Alice, "but do you know who she was and why we chose that name for you?"

"No, I don't, Mama," answered Ella honestly.

"Well, Saint Elizabeth was a very special person," began Princess Alice. "She did everything she could to help the poor. She was a rich young lady who lived a long time ago. She was married to a handsome young man named Prince Ludwig of Thuringen. She spent her time going to banquets and enjoying life, until one day her life changed. She was on her way to a feast when she happened to see a poor beggar freezing in the snow by the side of the road. This made Saint Elizabeth very sad, and she decided to give her warm, beautiful cloak to the poor man.

"From that moment on, she began to help needy people more and more. Once, she saw a man with leprosy in the street and brought him to her house. She washed his sores, fed him a meal, and let him sleep in her own bed. Can you imagine doing that? When Elizabeth's husband, Ludwig, came home, he was angry and disgusted to see the sick man in the bed. Suddenly, though, God showed Ludwig that the leper was exactly like Christ crucified. He was suffering and rejected just like Christ on the cross. After that, Ludwig did everything he could to help Ella in her charity works. Several years later, the prince died, and Saint Elizabeth left the beautiful palace where she lived. She sold all her luxurious clothes, furniture, dishes, and artwork and used the money to feed the hungry and start hospitals for the poor. She took care of many patients herself, even when she felt ill and weak."

Princess Alice paused and looked at Ella. "Now why do you think we named you after Saint Elizabeth?"

Ella shook herself. She had been so caught up in her mother's story that for a moment she had forgotten why her mother had begun to tell it. She thought hard for a while.

"Well," Ella said slowly, "I think you want me to be like her. You want me to care about the poor."

Princess Alice gave Ella a warm hug. "You're exactly right, my dear. I know that sometimes it's much more fun to play with your sister or friends rather than do works of charity. Remember, though, that we must try to be like Saint Elizabeth and show love to those who are poor or suffering."

"I understand, Mama," answered Ella.

"I knew you would," smiled Princess Alice. "Now why don't you wash up and get ready for bed. I'll send Nurse in with some warm milk for you. It's very chilly tonight."

As she lay in bed a little while later, Ella prayed that she might help others as Saint Elizabeth had so long ago. Years later, in a country far away from her native Hesse, Ella's prayer would be answered.

Chapter Two

On a beautiful May day in 1870, Ella, her mother, and her great-aunt, Empress Marie of Russia, relaxed on the terrace of a sprawling castle near the Rhine River. A tangy citrus smell wafted toward them from the lime trees growing in large pots on the terrace. In the distance they could see the sparkling blue of the flowing river.

"It is always so pleasant here," sighed Empress Marie. "I wish we could visit more often."

Empress Marie was Ella's father's aunt. She had married the emperor of Russia, Alexander II, and lived most of the year in St. Petersburg, Russia. Every summer, though, she and her sons came to visit her brother, Prince Alexander, at his big estate in Heilegenberg. Ella always felt a little shy around the richly dressed empress, who traveled with nearly one hundred courtiers and servants.

Despite her wealth, Empress Marie always seemed a little sad to young Ella.

"Ella, why don't you come on a walk with me?" asked a boy's voice. "I found some beautiful flowers we can look at."

Ella stood up with excitement and turned toward the voice. A tall, dark boy with serious eyes stood on the stone steps leading up to the terrace. He was Grand Duke Serge, Empress Marie's son. Even though the boy was several years older than she, he often took breaks from playing ball with the other boys to spend quiet time with young Ella.

After receiving her mother's permission to leave, Ella and Serge set out to explore Prince Alexander's vast gardens. A series of paths wound through colorful flowerbeds and past stately old trees. Ella and Serge shared a love of nature and often stopped to admire the bright plants all around them. One of Ella's favorite pastimes was sketching nature scenes.

"I wish I had brought my sketchpad today," she commented to Serge. "The roses look so beautiful."

"They do indeed," Serge agreed. "Uncle Alexander's gardens are almost as impressive as those at Peterhof," he said, referring to one of the Russian imperial family's spectacular palaces.

"I'm sure that Peterhof must be lovely," sighed Ella. "I hope I will see it someday."

"I hope you will too, Ella," said Serge.

A short two months after her walk with Serge, Ella was to remember that happy afternoon and wish that she could go back in time. By July 15, war with the French had broken out in her country and she and her family were living in fear. Ella did not really understand why the Franco-Prussian War had begun, but she knew that the fighting was dangerously close by.

"Don't be afraid children, we'll be home soon," Princess Alice said serenely. She and her children were crammed into a coach riding through the streets of Darmstadt on their way to the family's palace. Despite her mother's calm tone, Ella could tell that Princess Alice was feeling anxious. Outside the closed windows of their coach, chaos reigned in the streets of the city. Peeking out her window, Ella saw misery everywhere. Crowds of the poor gathered outside soup kitchens hoping for a bite to eat. The streets and parks of the city were crammed with French prisoners of war. The wounded were lying down wherever they could, moaning piteously.

"This is an impossible situation," Princess Alice snapped, studying the scene outside. "Relief must be organized immediately." Ella knew that her energetic mother would make good on her words. Princess Alice could not stand to see people suffering and would do what she could to help everyone, even the enemy soldiers.

"I wish Papa were here," said little Irene tearfully. "I would feel safer."

"Papa must do his duty and lead our soldiers," said Princess Alice, giving the little girl a squeeze. Prince Louis, Ella's father, had left the previous week to lead his regiment in battle. As the children waved goodbye to their father, Ella wondered whether she would ever see him again.

Almost as soon as the family settled into the palace in Darmstadt, Princess Alice set to work to help those suffering all around them. Though she was pregnant and constantly tired, the princess somehow found the strength to organize three military hospitals. She and her daughters went themselves to visit the wounded and try to bring them comfort. Princess Alice also collected food, blankets, clothing, and medicine to be sent to the soldiers fighting at the front.

"I'm so worried about Mama," said Ella one day as she and Victoria sat knitting woolen socks for soldiers. "She needs to rest or she might get really ill."

"I know," agreed Victoria. "The baby will be born soon and she needs to save her strength."

"Ouch!" exclaimed Ella, shaking her cramped hand. "I really don't like knitting." She put down the lumpy gray sock she had been struggling with and tried not to notice the smooth, neat one that Victoria was expertly knitting.

Ella walked over to the large window in their room and gazed out into the garden. It was no longer a beautiful oasis filled with colorful flowers. Instead, the plants and bushes had been trampled and the grass ground down into mud. About fifty military tents were crowded into the garden, and all around them sat or stood wounded French soldiers. Some were missing arms or legs, and others were so heavily bandaged they looked like mummies. But, amazingly, the men seemed cheerful. All day and into the night the girls heard the sounds of French folk songs and loud laughter as the soldiers gathered around small campfires. It had been Princess Alice's idea to set up the barracks in their garden, because the city of Darmstadt was running out of space to house all the French prisoners.

The men living in Ella's garden were the lucky ones.

Princess Alice made sure that they were well fed and given the medical care they needed. Ella had heard the family's cook complain bitterly that while Princess Alice's household tightened their belts and ate thin soups for their meals, the soldiers were given meat and bread to build their strength. When one of her children whined about being hungry, Princess Alice would tell them to remember the Good Samaritan who had helped his enemy. "God will reward us for helping these poor men," she told the children.

One chilly October day, Ella, Victoria, and Irene sat playing cards in the nursery. It was hard to concentrate on the game, because right at that moment their mother was giving birth in another room of the palace. On the table next to them, baked apples cooled on plates. None of the girls had any appetite. Suddenly, a servant girl burst excitedly into the room.

"Come, girls!" she exclaimed. "Your mother wishes to see you!"

The girls rushed into the hallway and up the stairs to their mother's room. Ella and Victoria approached Princess Alice shyly as she lay exhausted on her bed. Next to her curled a little bundle that was whimpering quietly. Princess Alice gave them a tired smile.

"Well, girls," she said, "come and take a look at little Frederick."

The girls approached the little bundle and peered carefully into a tiny red face.

"He's . . . very cute, Mama," offered Victoria uncertainly.

"That's all right, Victoria," smiled Princess Alice. "I know he's not very handsome now, but he'll improve with time."

After the birth of their brother, time seemed to go by quickly until a joyful early spring day in March.

"The war is over!" shouted Victoria one morning as she burst into the nursery. The children all hugged each other. "Papa will be home soon!" exclaimed little Irene as she clapped her hands.

That night, every house in Darmstadt, from the humblest shack to the royal palace, burned candles in its windows to celebrate the end of the war. Later in the month, the children were overjoyed when Prince Louis returned home. Thin and tired, he nevertheless found the energy to gather the children round him and entertain them with stories of battles and bravery. Prussia's highest medal of honor was pinned to his chest. Ella was always to remember the relief she felt when the war was over. She was also to remember forever the lesson her mother had taught her by her kindness to the French prisoners of war: "Love your enemies, do good, and lend, expecting nothing in return; and your reward will be great." *

---

* Luke 6:35

Chapter Three

ifteen-year-old Ella stood nervously before the mirror in the bedroom she shared with Victoria. She frowned at her reflection, displeased. No one else would have found anything to criticize in her steady gray eyes, clear skin, and light hair arranged in fashionable rolls at the back of her head. But Ella was preparing for a ball, and though she approved of the small white flowers clustered becomingly in her hair, she couldn't say the same of her dress. The simple gray silk was gathered at the bodice and then draped over a white underdress. One small bow decorated the neckline. Ella knew that the dress, made over from last year, would not be nearly as elegant as those worn by other girls at tonight's ball. Frustrated, she pulled on a pair of hand-me-down white gloves. Sometimes it was difficult not having money to buy the attractive clothes other girls took for granted.

"Ella, it's almost time to leave," called Victoria excitedly from the doorway. She was already draped in a heavy wine-colored cape.

"I'm coming," answered Ella as she reached for the green shawl she would wear outside.

As she and Victoria hurried down the steps toward their father's carriage, her spirits began to lift. A ball was always exciting, even if one's dress was not the most beautiful in the room. She glanced up at the palace windows to see her younger sister Alix gazing wistfully down at her and Victoria.

A half-hour later, the girls walked into a glittering ballroom filled with waltzing couples. Ella and Victoria curtseyed politely to their hostess and then turned eagerly to greet their friends who had already arrived. Ella was chatting happily with a friend when a young man approached her.

"Elizabeth," said a whining male voice, "I would very much like to dance with you." Ella turned reluctantly toward the young man standing next to her. His face, red from the heat of the room, was unattractively ringed with bristling sideburns. He turned so that his arm, which hung limply at his side, was hidden from view. Poor William, thought Ella, why is he so ashamed of that arm?

"Certainly," she answered him, "I would be delighted." Ella felt a little guilty for expressing pleasure that she didn't feel at all. Prince William of Prussia was probably the last man in the room that she cared to dance with. Not only was he an awkward dancer, but he liked to talk only about himself, bragging about his skills at hunting and shooting. Ella knew that William was in love with her and wanted to marry her. If she married him, Ella would have great wealth and power. She also knew, however, that she could never love such a conceited man.

After dancing with William, Ella thanked him politely and then escaped to the other side of the ballroom. She hid behind a large bouquet of white lilies to catch her breath. As soon as she ventured back onto the dance floor, a young Englishman in a tight waistcoat approached her eagerly and asked her for a waltz. The rest of the evening passed in a delightful blur as Ella danced with a succession of officers, all of whom gazed at her with admiring eyes. Though modest Ella would never have believed it, she was considered to be the prettiest girl in Darmstadt society.

Later that spring, Ella and a group of friends, including Prince William, gathered in the city park for a planned walk in the woods. The young people stood in a chattering group, the girls clutching their straw hats to keep them from fluttering away in the strong, fresh breeze. Nearby stood their chaperone, Miss Helen. No mixed group of girls and young men could spend time together unless they were accompanied by a respectable older lady. Miss Helen watched the group carefully through her thick spectacles to make sure no one was flirting and that no couple tried to separate themselves from the others.

"Let's get started!" called out Victoria. "It's a beautiful day!"

The young people scampered eagerly up a small incline toward the woods. Huffing and puffing a little behind the group trudged Prince William. He tried vainly to catch up with Ella, who strode ahead clutching her sketchpad and pencil box.

"Ella!" he called out crossly. "Wait for me!"

Ella pretended she didn't hear him for a minute or two, but then began to feel she was being unkind. Annoyed, she slowed down so that Prince William could catch up with her.

"Ella, why have you been avoiding me?" asked William in a hurt tone. "Didn't you receive my letter?"

Ella didn't know what to say. She had in fact received William's letter, the latest of many. The trouble was that she didn't know how to respond to them. The letters were all flowery love notes declaring William's devotion to her. She didn't want to hurt him, but at the same time had no intention of encouraging him in the idea that she would one day marry him.

"William," Ella stammered, "I have indeed received your kind letters, and I am most flattered by their sentiments, but as I am still very young . . ."

"Young!" he scoffed. "You are sixteen already!"

"Well, yes," Ella admitted, "but you must remember that I am still grieving for dear Mama and May." Ella's voiced choked a little as she said the words. Though she was using grief as an excuse to keep William at bay, her sad feelings were very real. The previous year had seen a great tragedy in her family. Both Princess Alice and Ella's younger sister May had died of diphtheria. With typical courage, Princess Alice had nursed the children who were sick with the dread disease. Though Victoria, Irene, and Ernest had all recovered, their mother and little May were too weak to fight the infection, and both had died.

"Ah yes," responded William, a bit embarrassed, "it's understandable that your thoughts should be elsewhere."

"Yes indeed," replied Ella firmly, as she excused herself and rushed ahead to rejoin the rest of the group.

Later that day, Ella and Victoria sat out in the family garden sipping lemonade. A wonderful scent of roses and jasmine filled the air as the girls chatted quietly.

"Well, Ella," Victoria was saying with a smile, "I can certainly understand why you're not interested in William. He is hardly a Prince Charming. In fact, he is closer to a troll, if truth be told!"

"Oh, Victoria," protested Ella, though she couldn't help giggling, "we mustn't say cruel things about poor William. What would Mama say if she were here?"

"She would assure you that the choice of whom to marry is yours alone. She and Papa always agreed about this."

Ella felt better when she heard Victoria's words. It was true that her parents had always told their daughters that they would be able to choose their own husbands. This was unusual freedom for royal princesses of their time, who were often married off to men they barely knew.

Over the next year, Ella continued her whirlwind of parties and social events. She danced and talked with many handsome young men, but did not feel drawn to any in particular. She felt cheerful and lighthearted most of the time, though she never wholly forgot her mother or May. At times, when she thought of her mother's serious but kind face, she felt a little guilty. Neither Ella nor her sisters did as much charitable work as they had done when their mother was alive. Occasionally Ella, Victoria, and Alix would visit a hospital or sew clothing for the poor, but not as frequently as in the past. Sometimes Ella pictured her mother gazing down on them sorrowfully from heaven, wondering if her daughters were straying from the true Christian path.

Around this time, Ella became reacquainted with her cousin Serge. The two had been good friends when Ella was a child but hadn't seen each other in quite a few years. At first Ella didn't think much of Serge. He seemed cold and reserved, and though he was developing strong feelings for Elizabeth, he didn't show them. Ella and Victoria decided that Serge and his brother were snobs and not worth thinking about.

Late in 1882, however, Serge visited Hesse again, and this time Ella felt differently about him. Both of Serge's parents had died in the last two years. Serge's father, Emperor Alexander II, had been assassinated in Russia only a year after his mother, Empress Marie, had died. Ella's warm heart ached for the young man's loss. She felt that since both of them had lost parents, they now had an important experience in common. When Serge came to visit her at the palace in Darmstadt, she went out of her

way to be friendly and try to cheer her depressed cousin. One morning they went for a walk together in the palace garden.

"I'm so glad that you enjoyed your trip to Italy," Ella was saying. "I had a wonderful time in Venice when I visited."

"Yes," said Serge gloomily, "the art of Titian was something of a comfort after the disasters of these past few years."

"Oh! Are you an admirer of his paintings? I was so moved by his *Assumption of the Virgin.* If only I could paint something one-tenth as splendid," exclaimed Ella excitedly. "Victoria and I gazed at the painting open-mouthed for a half-hour at least. The museum guard was becoming annoyed with us. I believe he thought we were planning to steal the canvas!"

Ella and Serge both loved art and could discuss Italian painters in particular for hours at a time. Serge showed a flattering interest in Ella's sketching, though she dismissed her own work as "schoolgirl doodling."

"Titian is truly able to capture the sublime spirit of the saints," commented Serge. "He and the great Raphael inspire in me an immediate desire to pray."

"In me also," agreed Ella. "The Virgin's face in Titian's painting expresses such holiness!"

Though Ella and Serge were of different religions—he was Orthodox and she Lutheran—they were both pious Christians. This was another bond that drew them together. Though Ella did not know much about the Orthodox faith, she respected Serge for his regular church-going.

"This was indeed a pleasant afternoon, Ella," said Serge shyly as he and Ella walked back toward the palace. "Thank you for distracting me with all this wonderful talk of art."

"Don't speak as if I were performing a tiresome duty," scolded Ella playfully. "I enjoyed our talk also. It made me long to visit Italy again!"

"Perhaps one day we will travel there together," suggested Serge, looking at her intensely.

Ella blushed. "That would indeed be lovely," she said as she pretended to examine a rose next to the garden path.

Later that day, after Serge had left, Ella thought deeply about their conversation. It seemed to her that Serge's attentiveness was becoming more and more serious. Her own feelings were becoming stronger also. At first, Serge's dark and brooding manner had displeased her. She had thought him cold. Now, though, Ella began to see her cousin as something of a romantic hero. He reminded her of Mr. Darcy in Jane Austen's *Pride and Prejudice*. In Austen's novel, the heroine, Elizabeth, also had grown to see beyond the hero's stiff exterior.

Ella's warm feelings for Serge were not shared by many others in her family. Victoria continued to see him as tiresome and snobbish, and Ella's grandmother, Queen Victoria of Great Britain, made it plain that she was opposed to any marriage between her granddaughter and the Russian grand duke. Queen Victoria was concerned because she had seen how unhappy Empress Marie, Ella's great-aunt, had been in Russia. Ella's grandmother much preferred that she marry someone like the Grand Duke Frederick of Baden. He was a pleasant young man who everyone felt would make a wonderful husband for Ella. However, when Frederick proposed to Ella in the winter of 1883, she gently refused him. By then she was sure that the man she wanted to marry was her cousin Serge.

When Serge visited Darmstadt again in September, he and Ella spent a great deal of time together walking and talking. When he finally found the courage to propose to her, Ella felt torn. She wanted to accept, but at the same time she did not want to displease her family. Confused, Ella refused Serge's offer of marriage. He felt very hurt and left for Russia soon afterward. Ella realized immediately how much she missed her cousin and how

much she had grown to care for him. She decided to risk her grandmother's disapproval and agree to marry Serge. After praying to God for guidance, she sat down, took a deep breath, and wrote a letter of acceptance to the grand duke. She would marry Serge and move to a strange new land called Russia.

Chapter Four

Ella, nervous and excited, tried to sit still as a sharp pin was thrust into her elaborately piled hair. "Ouch!" she exclaimed under her breath as yet another one poked into her scalp. It was hard to believe that the period of her engagement had flown by and she was now dressing for her wedding. "If I have the strength to walk into the chapel!" she thought secretly. Ella's shoulders and back already ached from the weight of the clothes she would wear for the ceremony. Her dress of heavy silver cloth scratched her skin and the matching train made her feel as if stones were sewn into the cloth. She thought the diamond necklace around her neck looked beautiful, but the cherry-sized diamond earrings she wore dug painfully into her ears. "I wonder if anyone would notice if I slipped them off?" she thought mischievously. She knew that would be impossible, since around her stood a small army of ladies-in-waiting ready to pull and prod at Ella's clothing if needed.

At last the court hairdresser grunted that his creation was finished. "My hair looks like a creampuff about to explode!" thought Ella critically as she examined her teased and curled tresses in a mirror. Sighing, she turned as her sister-in-law, Empress Marie, attached a lace veil and crown to her head. Feeling as if she were balancing ten books on her head that could topple at any minute, Ella began her slow walk toward the palace chapel.

It was only a few weeks ago that she and her family had boarded the train in Darmstadt for their trip to St. Petersburg, Russia. As Ella waved goodbye to the friends who had come to the station to see her off, she felt sadness sweeping over her. When would she see her homeland again? Luckily, Victoria sensed Ella's mood and pulled her away from the window.

"Why don't we go to the dining car and order lunch?" she asked cheerfully. "I'm famished!"

"Me too," answered Ella.

The two young women walked arm-in-arm through the rumbling train. Both wore practical gray traveling dresses that would hide any dust from the long journey to come. At last they reached the dining car and sat down at a small table. A busy waiter took their order, and then Victoria took Ella's hand.

"I know you're nervous, Ella," she said kindly, "but everything will be fine. I assure you that marriage is wonderful." Victoria had married Prince Louis of Battenberg a few months earlier and was still glowing with happiness. She and her husband, an officer in the British Royal Navy, both loved travel and adventure.

"I know you're right, Victoria," answered Ella, "but I can't help feeling upset about grandmother's disapproval." Queen Victoria of Great Britain had written Ella that she was not happy with her choice of a husband.

"Well," said Victoria, "she will grow used to the idea. I have come to see that Serge has good qualities, though I used to think him a true stick-in-the-mud!" Ella was not hurt by Victoria's words. The sisters were always honest with each other.

"Well, at least Alix has no worries!" laughed Ella as she pointed at her younger sister. Twelve-year-old Alix was so excited about the train adventure that she was hopping up and down the dining car, trying to peer out the windows at the passing countryside. After she nearly knocked into a waiter, Alix's governess called to her in an irritated tone to sit down and act like a proper young lady.

The next day their train reached the Russian border,

and the family boarded a special imperial train that would take them the rest of the way. The luxurious train was filled with vases of white flowers as a tribute from Serge to Ella. He knew that white was her favorite color. The train at last stopped at Peterhof near the Baltic Sea. Serge greeted Ella on the train platform.

"I am so happy to see you, my dear!" he greeted her in accented English. His face looked unusually relaxed and happy.

"I have made the right decision!" thought Ella as Serge kissed her hand. They stepped together into a sumptuous gilt carriage along with Serge's brother, Emperor Alexander III, and his wife, Empress Marie. Nervous, Ella bowed her head toward the pair but was surprised to be enveloped in a warm hug by the huge emperor. "Call me Sasha!" he exclaimed. "After all, we are almost family!"

"Look how you have frightened her, Sasha!" scolded his wife, Marie. "I'm afraid that he does not know his own strength," smiled Marie at Ella. Ella felt comfortable immediately. Though "Sasha" was ruler over the largest nation on earth, he seemed more like a huge playful bear than a powerful emperor.

At last the line of carriages pulled up in front of the most magnificent palace Ella had ever seen. As they drove up to the building, she saw a vision out of a fairy tale. An enormous fountain rose in steps up to the façade of the grand palace, which seemed to stretch a mile into the distance. The fountain was lined on either side by golden statues that sparkled in the summer sun. As they entered the palace, Ella glimpsed beautiful gardens laid out on either side of the building. She longed to wander about the grounds with her sketchpad, but felt too shy to ask.

Instead, she and her sisters were given a formal tour of the palace.

"I'm too afraid to touch anything lest I break it," whispered Alix to Ella.

"Yes," agreed Ella, "it seems more like a home for gods and goddesses than for mere mortals."

A few days later, the wedding guests left Peterhof by train for St. Petersburg. Again, Ella was stunned by the opulence of the Winter Palace, where she was to be married. The huge palace boasted hundreds of rooms filled with priceless art and glittering with crystal chandeliers and shining gilt stuccoed walls. The next morning, as if in a dream, Ella found herself being dressed ("like a doll," she thought) for her wedding. Followed by anxious ladies-in-waiting and Empress Marie, she walked toward the palace chapel. She passed through several ornate rooms lined by marble columns and hung with portraits. Ella felt the eyes in the paintings were watching her sympathetically as she nervously tried not to trip over her heavy skirts.

Ella entered the chapel slowly and with dignity. The church's white walls and gilt carvings sparkled as they reflected the many candles burning throughout the room. On either side of the chapel, finely dressed men and women turned to look at her. Many of the faces expressed admiration at Ella's beauty. Empress Marie gave Ella an encouraging smile and turned to join the other guests. Taking a deep breath, Ella took her place next to Serge. He looked unusually handsome in his military uniform. A tall wedding candle was placed in both their hands. In front of them, a bearded priest began to recite a long litany in Slavonic, the ancient Slavic church language.

31

Later, Ella and Serge were led to the middle of the chapel. Behind them, several of Serge's fellow military officers took turns holding heavy gold crowns over the couple's heads. Through a kind of dreamy haze, Ella heard the priest asking her:

"Do you, Elizabeth, have a good, free, and unconstrained will and a firm intention to take as your husband this man, Serge, whom you see here before you?"

"I have, reverend father," she answered with a beating heart.

"Have you promised yourself to any other man?" the priest asked.

"I have not promised myself, reverend father," Ella answered.

The rest of the ceremony flew by as she and Serge sipped together from a common cup and processed in a circle around the central lectern to the beautiful hymn, "Rejoice, O Isaiah!" After the service finished, Ella and Serge entered a nearby drawing room for a short Lutheran marriage ceremony. Next, the couple left to be guests of honor at a magnificent feast held in the palace concert hall. By the end of the evening, Ella's shoulders and back ached as if she had been lifting heavy weights. "Only an hour or so left," Ella thought as she smiled politely at yet another guest being introduced to her.

At last she and Serge were free to leave for Serge's private palace on Nevsky Prospect, St. Petersburg's main avenue. A few days later they left for the first part of their honeymoon, which they would spend in the city of Moscow. Early one morning, they boarded the train together.

"Well," said Serge as he settled back into the upholstered

seat of their private compartment, "at last we are escaping the crowds of well-wishers."

"Until we reach Moscow, of course," agreed Ella. "Everyone has been so kind, but I must admit that it's pleasant to be alone for once."

"Indeed," said Serge as he opened a newspaper to read.

Ella sometimes wished that Serge were more talkative. Since the wedding, they had been constantly busy with events and parties and were almost never alone together. The train trip to Moscow seemed an ideal time to have a heart-to-heart conversation, but Serge did not seem to want to talk. Ella sighed, but decided to make the best of the trip and the coming visit to Moscow.

Once they arrived in the ancient city, Serge and Ella visited many of the beautiful, famous churches there. Ella thought the colorful churches with their bright gold onion domes were stunning, but some things about the Orthodox faith confused her. When she and Serge entered a church, he would always venerate the icons, crossing himself and solemnly kissing each holy picture. Ella thought this was strange. "How can Serge actually kiss the saints' pictures?" she thought to herself. "It is wrong to worship anything except God Himself." As a Lutheran, Ella had been taught that venerating holy images was something like

33

worshiping idols. Ella decided to show respect to the icons by curtseying in front of them, but she did not feel comfortable kissing them. Later, as she learned more about Orthodoxy, her feelings would change.

After spending time in Moscow, Ella and Serge left for Ilinskoye. This was Serge's country estate ten miles outside the city. From the first moment Ella saw the old, beautiful home, she fell in love with it. The peaceful countryside was soothing, and she and Serge enjoyed going on walks in the birch woods near the house. Sometimes they collected mushrooms, a favorite Russian pastime.

The one thing that disturbed Ella about their country home was the difficult life of the peasants who lived in the neighboring village of Ilinskoye. When she visited the village for the first time, she was shocked by the broken-down cabins in which most of the people lived. "How can they keep warm in such houses during the winter?" she thought. She also saw that many of the men got drunk frequently because of their hard lives. Most had to work from dawn to nightfall in the fields, planting and later harvesting crops. The villagers did not have any of the modern farm equipment that Ella had seen back home in Hesse. Instead, they used old wooden ploughs that were not effective in turning up soil for planting. Most of all, Ella was saddened when she learned that there was no regular doctor in the village and that many babies died soon after birth because of the poor medical care.

One day as she and Serge ate breakfast on their veranda, Ella brought up an idea she had to make the villagers' lives easier.

"Serge, I really think that something needs to be done about the health care in Ilinskoye," she said. "Why, I heard yesterday that there is no proper midwife to help the women give birth!"

"Ella, Ella," answered Serge, "this is not Hesse. The peasants here are used to a hard life. They do not understand any other."

Ella felt herself getting a bit angry with her husband. "That may be true now," she said tartly, "but I believe it's our Christian duty to ease their suffering. When Mama first married Papa, there was no proper hospital in Hesse, but thanks to her there are now several. One must begin somewhere. I wish to at least hire a midwife for the village women."

Serge smiled indulgently at Ella as if she were asking for a new dress or parasol. "Well, if it will make you happy, I don't see why we can't do so. I will inquire about bringing a qualified woman from Moscow."

Ella was glad that she was able to help the villagers of Ilinskoye in even such a small way. Inside her a desire to help the poor and suffering was growing. More and more she remembered how her mother, Princess Alice, had spent her time aiding the less fortunate. It seemed that all of Mama's time was taken up with founding organizations that helped needy people, such as pregnant women, the insane, and the homeless. Ella began to realize that in Russia the needs of the poor were even greater than they had been in Hesse.

Chapter Five

Ella yawned behind her blue embroidered fan, hoping that no one around her would notice. She and Serge were seated in the white and gold imperial box at the famed Maryinsky Theater in St. Petersburg. Ella lifted her opera glasses to her eyes and looked down at the stage, where ballerinas in long diaphanous tutus whirled gracefully. She enjoyed the ballet but felt tired this evening.

"Ella, do you feel well, my dear?" asked Empress Marie kindly. Emperor Alexander III (or "Sasha" as the family called him) and the empress always attended the ballet with Ella and Serge.

"Oh yes, thank you, Minnie," answered Ella. Minnie was the empress's nickname. "It's just I'm a little tired tonight. Especially when I think that we still have the ball to attend!"

"Don't I know it," agreed Empress Marie. "How many boring ambassadors I shall have to make small talk with!"

Ella smiled at the empress's comment. She felt the same way. At most balls she attended, Ella had to spend much of her time talking to important guests from other countries. The diplomats were usually pompous old men who could talk for hours about medals they had been awarded or how much the monarch in their country depended on them. Ella loved to dance and took pleasure in dressing beautifully, but she didn't enjoy having to entertain so many people. Sometimes she wished that she could be an ordinary young woman instead of a grand duchess.

After she and Serge were first married, Ella had enjoyed all the parties and dinners that she was invited to. She loved putting on the pretty gowns she had never been able to afford at home in Hesse. Serge was very generous in giving her expensive jewels to wear. She felt like a fairy princess. Ella was admired by everyone for her charm and beauty. She quickly became the most popular hostess in St. Petersburg, and everyone longed to be invited to balls at Serge's Sergeievsky Palace. Ella enjoyed being so popular, but at the same time she began to feel that there was something empty in her lifestyle. She remembered guiltily that Princess Alice, her mother, had spent most of her time doing charity work rather than participating in the social whirl.

Just as these feelings were growing in Ella, an event happened that moved her much closer to a more spiritual life. She and Serge were asked by the emperor to go in his place to the Holy Land, where a large Orthodox church was being consecrated. It was built at the foot of the Mount of Olives and was dedicated to the former Empress Marie, Serge's mother. Ella and Serge made the long journey, and both were very moved by what they saw. Ella visited many of the places where Christ Himself had lived and taught. One day she and Serge took a walk through the cobbled streets of Bethlehem. They had just visited the Church of the Nativity. Ella had been very moved as she and Serge approached the hollowed nook in the church where Christ was born. They had knelt before the opening to what had been the simple cave and prayed silently.

"Oh, Serge, isn't it moving that we just saw Christ's actual birthplace?" sighed Ella.

"Yes," answered Serge, "it was humbling to see what a small cave it was."

"One can feel the holiness of the place," commented Ella. "I really felt the closeness of the Lord in that dark place. Serge," she went on shyly, "seeing the Church of St. Mary Magdalene yesterday made me realize once and for all that I would like to learn more about Orthodoxy. I was so moved by the beautiful singing. I truly felt as if I were among angels."

Serge turned to her with a happy expression. "Why, Ella, I had no idea that you were becoming interested in our faith."

"Over the last year, I have come to feel that the Orthodox Church is more prayerful and spiritual than my Lutheran faith," answered Ella seriously. "I think that Christ is calling me to explore your ancient church's teachings."

After Ella and Serge returned to Russia, she was true

to her word and began to read avidly about the Orthodox faith. Serge was very pleased and answered any questions about doctrine she had. Ella began to attend an Orthodox church with Serge and to pray using Orthodox prayers. Over time she decided that she would convert formally to Orthodoxy. She was overjoyed to join the Church. Her new faith led her to do more charity work. After a huge famine left thousands of peasants hungry in the countryside, Ella organized fundraisers that collected four hundred thousand rubles for the victims. She also traveled to the places where people were suffering most to make sure the money was spent properly.

Though Ella loved Russia and the many friends she had there, she often missed her family back in Darmstadt. Her favorite dream was that at least one family member would join her and move to Russia. That family member turned out to be her younger sister Alix. Ever since Alix and Serge's nephew, Nicholas, had joked and played together at Ella's wedding, Ella had been hoping that the two would one day marry. Finally, in 1894, Ella got her wish. It had taken Alix a long time to consent to Nicholas's proposals because she was a devout Lutheran. In order to marry Nicholas, the future tsar of Russia, she would have to become Orthodox. After Ella became Orthodox, she spent a lot of time convincing Alix that true Christianity was only found in the Orthodox Church. At last Alix decided that Ella was right and consented to marry Nicholas.

Everyone was happily celebrating the couple's engagement when a sudden tragedy took place. Emperor Alexander III had always been a healthy man, but suddenly he fell ill with nephritis, a disease of the kidneys. Within months, Ella's beloved friend was dead. The family was overcome with sadness, but Nicholas, who would now become emperor, decided that he wanted to marry Alix on their planned wedding date. He felt that he needed a wife's support as he began the hard task of ruling Russia. One afternoon, Alix (who was now called Alexandra after her conversion) and Ella sat together in a sitting room of the Winter Palace.

"I am so sorry, Sunny," said Ella, calling Alexandra by her childhood nickname, "it is a sad way to begin your new life here."

"I don't know if I am ready to be an empress, Ella," said Alexandra tearfully. "I thought I would have years to prepare before Nicky and I would become rulers." Ella nodded sympathetically. She knew that Alexandra was very shy. While Ella was comfortable meeting new people and was a skilled hostess, Alexandra often froze in social situations. People mistakenly thought she was cold and snobbish, while actually she was terribly nervous with strangers.

"We will all help you, Alexandra," Ella assured her sister while warmly grasping her hand. "It will just take practice. Everyone will love you when they get to truly know your character. Now," she continued briskly, "let us begin to plan your wedding."

Despite Ella's hard work, the wedding was depressingly different from her own of years earlier. It took place on a gray November day with all the guests still saddened by Emperor Alexander III's death. No cheering crowds stood outside the Winter Palace as they had for Ella's and Serge's wedding. No sumptuous reception followed the ceremony. Poor Alexandra almost fainted from stress and from having to wear the heavy court wedding dress. More than anything else, she was glad when the ordeal was over.

The next ten years passed quietly for Ella. As she grew more and more serious about her Orthodox faith, she spent more time in prayer and charity work and less in society. She began to prefer life at their country home, Ilinskoye, over life in the glamorous world of St. Petersburg. She spent most of her summers at Ilinskoye, caring for Serge's nephew Dmitri and niece Marie. The children's mother had died suddenly and their father, Grand Duke Paul, needed help raising the boy and girl.

While Ella's life was peaceful, life in Russia was becoming dangerous. Groups of radical students and revolutionaries were angry because many of Russia's peasants and workers were poor and at times hungry. However, instead of working peacefully to help the poor, the revolutionaries turned to violence. Many government officials were assassinated by the revolutionaries, even those who were trying to help the peasants have a better life.

Because of all this violence, Ella worried greatly about the safety of her husband. Though he had recently retired from his position as governor of Moscow, Ella knew that Serge was still in danger. Serge said that he was not afraid of the revolutionaries.

"Ella, my dear," Serge said one afternoon in February 1905 as he and she sat together, "please stop worrying. Those men are too cowardly to attack me here in Moscow, where the police watch our home. If anything, they will try to shoot me at Ilinskoye, where they have a good chance of escaping after killing me. I'm just joking!" Serge assured Ella as he saw her shocked face. "I'm sure I will be here for years to come!" He kissed her goodbye and prepared to leave the house.

Ella watched Serge through her bedroom window as he walked toward his coach parked outside. All day she had been feeling nervous and afraid, though she didn't know why. She turned from the window toward her embroidery frame, hoping that sewing would take her mind off things. Just as she picked up her needle, a huge explosion shook the house. Terrified, Ella ran downstairs. She threw open the front door and ran to the end of the street. The broken remains of Serge's carriage lay about in the street and a great amount of blood was staining the white snow red. In front of the bloody scene stood a wild-eyed man, held on either side by policemen.

"Down with the damned tsar! Down with the cursed government!" the man yelled as he was taken away.

Horrified, Ella looked around her for Serge but noticed only a dismembered arm in the snow. Without thinking, she stooped to pick it up and held it to her. By this time a crowd had gathered and people were gazing at Ella, wide-eyed and terrified.

"Don't stare like that!" she almost snapped. "Please, someone help that poor man who is gravely injured!"

Serge's coach driver, Rudinkin, was lying on the snow, bleeding from several large gashes. A sleigh was quickly brought and Rudinkin was rushed to the hospital.

The next few hours passed in a blur for Ella. Not caring what people thought, she knelt in the snow to gather whatever pieces of Serge's body she could find, placing them gently on a stretcher. A group of soldiers carried the stretcher, covered by an army coat, to the nearby Monastery of the Miracle. Ella knelt before the stretcher in her bloodstained blue dress as a priest read prayers for the dead. Everyone in the church admired how strong and calm Ella appeared.

Later that evening Ella visited Rudinkin, the injured coachman, in the hospital. The poor man kept asking if Grand Duke Serge was all right, and Ella assured him that he was. Rudinkin died later that night at peace, thinking that Serge had survived the blast. After attending a service for Serge the next morning, Ella prayed for a long while and decided to take a courageous step. She would

visit the man who had murdered her husband and encourage him to repent of his horrible deed. Serge had always been concerned about the souls of those who died without confessing their sins.

Ella drove to the Taganka Prison in a carriage covered in black mourning crepe. The prison guards did not want to allow her to see Serge's murderer, but Ella insisted. Serge's murderer's name was Kalayev. He was a college student from Warsaw, Poland. Kalayev was a sensitive poet who had become a revolutionary because he thought it was the only way to bring justice to Russia. Sadly, he was so full of hate that he thought only killing people would help the poor of Russia have a better life.

Covered in a black veil, Ella entered Kalayev's prison cell.

"Who are you?" he asked.

"I am the wife of the man whom you have killed," Ella answered.

"It is useless for you to come," said Kalayev.

"You must have suffered so much to have committed this terrible act," Ella stated.

Kalayev became upset and began a long angry speech about how killing Serge was a just act. He said that if he had gone to talk to Serge about the misery of the poor in Russia, the grand duke would have ignored him.

"As for myself," Kalayev shouted fanatically, "I would give a thousand lives, not one, if only Russia could be free!" [*]

* Saint Elizabeth's conversation with Kalayev is reproduced as it truly happened. Kalayev recounted the conversation to his fellow revolutionary, Savinkov. Savinkov later wrote the conversation down in his memoirs. St. Elizabeth also told of the conversation to her sister, Victoria, and to her brother.

Realizing that Kalayev was too stubborn to listen to anyone who disagreed with his ideas, Ella stood up and quietly handed him a small icon.

"I came to tell you that he forgives you," Ella stated with emotion. "I beg you to accept this little icon in his memory. I shall pray for you." She then quickly left the prison cell.

That night after her evening prayers, Ella lay down exhausted on her bed. She still felt numb and knew that the reality of Serge's death would take a while to truly sink in. She knew that after this tragedy she could never go back to her former life. Never again would she feel comfortable going to fancy balls or expensive restaurants. She wanted the rest of her life to be dedicated to Christ and His Church. At that moment, Ella knew that she wanted to become a nun.

Chapter Six

Elizabeth (she used her full name now that she was planning to become a nun) stood quietly in the front entrance of the Nicholas Palace in Moscow. It was the home where she and Serge had spent so much time during the years that he was governor of Moscow. Unfortunately, it would now always remind her of the terrible day when he was killed by a terrorist bomb. Elizabeth felt a little better when she reminded herself that she would never again have to enter the palace. In fact, she would never again enter any of the palaces she and Serge had owned. Now that Elizabeth was determined to become a nun, she had given all her properties to her niece, Marie, and nephew, Dmitri. Remembering Christ's words, "If you would be perfect,

47

go, sell what you possess and give to the poor, and you will have treasure in heaven; and come, follow Me," * Elizabeth had done just that. She had sold all her beautiful clothing, jewelry, and artwork and used the money to help the poor. All of her many servants had been given pensions and gone to work for other families. Only her personal maid, Barbara, remained with her.

Dressed in a simple gray gown and dark cloak, Elizabeth walked purposefully down the steps of the Nicholas Palace and climbed into her carriage. Behind her scurried Barbara, carrying one small suitcase of clothing. The two women were on their way to a new life. As the carriage rumbled over the bumpy road, Elizabeth turned to Barbara.

"Well, my faithful friend," she said cheerfully, "there is no turning back for me now, but you still have a chance for an easy life. Are you sure you would not like to go work for Countess Vera? She has asked me many times to send you to her. She is a kind lady."

"No, thank you, grand duchess," answered Barbara firmly. "Like you, I wish only to follow the Lord now. Besides, you will need my help."

"I will indeed," said Elizabeth seriously. "We have a lot of work before us."

The carriage soon turned into one of Moscow's main roads, the Great Ordinka. It passed the hospital Elizabeth had built years earlier. Then it stopped in front of a modest building not far from the hospital.

"Well, Barbara, here is our new home," said Elizabeth as she opened the door of the carriage and climbed out.

The two women entered the building and climbed a

---

* Matthew 19:21 RSV

worn staircase to the second floor. Elizabeth pulled a key from her bag and began to open the door of an apartment to their left. Across the hall, an elderly woman opened her door a crack and stared suspiciously at Elizabeth and Barbara. She obviously did not recognize Elizabeth in her plain clothes.

"Mind you don't make any noise at night," the old woman hissed. "I'm a bad sleeper."

"Please don't worry," answered Elizabeth humbly, "we are quiet people ourselves."

Their neighbor did not look convinced, but shut her door with an irritable snap. Elizabeth and Barbara entered the apartment and looked around. It was very different from the luxurious home they had just left. An old stove stood in the corner, and a few worn armchairs were arranged against the walls. A shabby rug that might once have had a pattern of flowers covered the floor.

"Well," said Elizabeth briskly, "this is our new home. Why don't we settle in?"

Barbara looked around doubtfully, but then set down the suitcase and rolled up her sleeves.

Ever since Serge's death, Elizabeth had spent almost every waking minute planning the convent she wished to build next to her hospital. The convent was to be named after Saints Mary and Martha, because Elizabeth wanted her nuns to be both prayerful and practical, like the sisters from the Bible. The nuns would spend most of their time helping the very poor of Moscow. Elizabeth also wanted to build a home for pregnant women, orphans, and people with severe handicaps.

In 1908, Elizabeth at last received permission from church authorities to begin her order of sisters. Two years later, on April 9, 1910, she and the convent's first group of sisters assembled in the main church dedicated to the Theotokos. They were to be tonsured nuns that day. The women in the church came from very different backgrounds. Some were rich and some were poor. Some were very educated and some could barely read. The one thing they had in common was their joyful desire to follow Christ and to spend their lives caring for Moscow's most suffering people.

Elizabeth stood before the crowded church, facing the sisters, and said, "I am about to leave the brilliant world in which it fell to me to occupy such a splendid position, but together with you I am about to enter a much greater world: that of the poor and afflicted." *

She then went with the other women who were to be tonsured nuns and stood by the icon of Christ at the front of the church. Like the other women, she stood with her head uncovered and her feet bare. The liturgy then began. Elizabeth, together with the other future nuns, was led to the bishop and asked, "Will you keep yourself in chastity, soberness, and piety?"

"Yes, Master, God helping me," she answered.

"Will you endure the difficulties of the poverty that belongs to the monastic life, for the sake of the kingdom of heaven?" the bishop went on.

"Yes, Master, God helping me," Elizabeth replied firmly.

As the service continued, the bishop prayed, "Behold, my children, the kind of promises you are giving to our Savior Christ, for angels are invisibly present, inscribing this profession of yours, for which you are also to be held accountable at the second coming of our Lord Jesus Christ. . . . Endure hardship as good soldiers of Christ, for although He is rich in mercy, He became poor for our sakes, coming among us that we might share in the riches of His kingdom."

Toward the end of the liturgy, each nun knelt before the bishop as he cut a section of her hair to symbolize the sacrifice she was making by giving up her worldly life and entering the convent. Next, the bishop covered each woman with a monastic habit, praying, "Our sister is clothed with the garment of gladness, in the name of the Father and of the Son and of the Holy Spirit." He also put sandals on her feet and a veil on her head. Finally, he handed each new nun a prayer rope, saying, "Sister, take the sword of the Spirit, which is the word of God, for continual prayer, in the name of the Father and of the Son and of the Holy Spirit."

After the liturgy finished, the bishop walked to the center of the church. Elizabeth approached him and bowed down three times. She was now to be blessed as abbess, or leader, of the new nuns and their convent. As she knelt down, Elizabeth felt both fear and joy. She was nervous when she thought that now she was responsible for the nuns present in the church. At the Last Judgment, Christ would ask her whether she had truly been a good mother to the women in her care. Elizabeth was happy, though, when she thought that at last she was following in her mother Alice's footsteps by dedicating her whole life to helping the needy. Elizabeth knew that her mother was looking down on her from heaven and was happy with what she saw.

The bishop placed his hand on Elizabeth's head and said in a deep voice, "Make this Your handmaid, Elizabeth, whom You have graciously pleased to set over this convent as abbess, worthy of Your goodness. Adorn her with all virtues, that through her own deeds she may offer a good example to those who are subject to her; that they, being moved to emulate her blameless life, may, with her, stand uncondemned before Your dread Judgment Seat." The bishop then handed Elizabeth a staff and a cross. Together these showed that she was to care for the convent sisters and to show them Christ's love, even when it meant painful sacrifice on her part.

Life at the Convent of Saints Mary and Martha was very busy. The sisters woke up at 6:00 A.M. and went to the hospital chapel for morning prayers. After prayers, they would drink tea and have a small breakfast. Next, they went to perform their "obediences," or jobs, for the day. Some nuns worked in the convent clinic, caring for patients free of charge. Some watched over the children in the convent orphanage or taught in the orphanage school. Four sisters were in charge of preparing meals for the poor in the convent cafeteria. About four hundred hungry people ate their meals there each day. Other sisters brought food directly to the homes of needy families. Two nuns organized a group of low-income women to sew clothing for poor children. Other nuns oversaw a special home for young women factory workers. The home was a safe haven for girls who would otherwise have to live in slum apartments and possibly turn to prostitution to survive.

The nuns ended their busy day with a light meal at 4:00 P.M. and Vespers and Matins at 5:00 P.M. The sisters gathered in the hospital chapel again at 9:00 P.M. for evening prayers. Elizabeth would personally bless each nun before she went back to her small "cell," or room, for bed.

One of Elizabeth's most important but also saddest duties was ministering to Moscow's very poorest in a slum called Khitrovka. This was an awful shantytown of twenty thousand people, full of crime and disease. Very few children born there lived to become adults. Elizabeth was very sad about the terrible lives of these children. She decided that she wanted to help as many of them as she could by taking them into her convent orphanage. In the orphanage, the children would receive enough food to eat and even go to school.

One day in July of 1913, Elizabeth and her former maid, the nun Barbara, got into the convent carriage and prepared to leave for Khitrovka. Outside the door of the carriage stood a red-faced, angry policeman.

"Your highness," the man spluttered, "I really must ask you again not to drive into that awful slum! We cannot protect you from so many criminals! Why, just last week four men were murdered in Khitrovka!"

"I know you are concerned, my dear Dmitri Pavlovich," answered Elizabeth calmly, "and I appreciate it. However, the Lord said, 'Do unto the least of these.'[*] It is our duty to help the poor children who cannot help themselves."

Before the policeman had time to continue his protests, Elizabeth gestured for the coachman to drive on. Before long, Mother Elizabeth and Sister Barbara began to notice an awful stench of cheap vodka, polluted water, and garbage. They were nearing Khitrovka. The carriage stopped at the outskirts of the slum, and Mother Elizabeth and Sister Barbara got out. Each carried large baskets of food, medicine, and bandages.

"I think we should try that house over there," said Mother Elizabeth, pointing at a broken-down shack across from them. Inside, a baby was wailing and a woman was cursing. Frightened, Sister Barbara followed Mother Elizabeth to the doorway. She didn't understand how the abbess could appear so calm and cheerful.

"Hello," called Mother Elizabeth as she peered into the dim hovel. "Two servants of Christ have stopped by to see if we can be of help to you." As Mother Elizabeth's eyes adjusted to the dark, she saw a miserable scene. A young girl of about seventeen stood in the center of the room. She was dressed in a ragged shift and an empty bottle dangled from her hand. Two little children cowered on a pile of dirty blankets in the corner. One looked about a year old and the other perhaps three. Both were painfully thin with large haunted eyes. Faded bruises were visible on their arms and legs.

"Matushka," said the girl in a raspy voice, "I did not

[*] Matthew 25:40

know it was you. Please come in." The people of Khitrovka were used to the sight of Mother Elizabeth. At first they thought it strange to see a nun, especially a former grand duchess. Now they were used to her and called her by the affectionate name "matushka," or "little mother."

Mother Elizabeth entered the filthy room and stood before the girl. "What is your name, my dear?" she asked.

"Pelagia," answered the girl. "And these brats are Katya and Tanya."

"They look like sweet children," said Mother Elizabeth. "Are you hungry, my dears?" She held out some bread rolls to the children. They looked at each other briefly and then rushed forward, grabbed the food, and wolfed it down.

"No manners at all," said Pelagia gruffly and cuffed Katya on the back of the head. The nuns winced at seeing this but tried not to look upset.

"Pelagia," said Mother Elizabeth carefully, "it seems that things here are quite difficult for you. Is there anything we can do to help? We have food and medicine."

"The only thing you could do is to take away these brats!" answered Pelagia. "My new boyfriend wants me to leave with him for Siberia. They have work logging. But he don't want the kids so I'm stuck." She glared at the children.

Mother Elizabeth and Sister Barbara exchanged glances. "You know, Pelagia," said Mother Elizabeth cautiously, "we have a special home for children at the convent. It's a lovely place. The children have plenty of food, clothes, even school." She paused. "Other mothers here in Khitrovka have asked me to let their children stay in the home. They can visit whenever they like," Mother

Elizabeth added quickly.

Pelagia stood quietly and seemed to think for a minute. "I know," she finally said, "Marusya told me the other day that Kirushka now lives with you. She even said you have a garden." Pelagia seemed to think some more and then suddenly burst out, "Take the brats! I don't want them anyway! They suck the life out of me!" She then rushed out of the hut as the children began to cry.

Mother Elizabeth and Sister Barbara quietly took the children's hands and led them out of the stinking shack. Little Katya was shaking and clung to Sister Barbara. The nuns noticed Pelagia sobbing quietly on a broken chair behind her shack. Mother Elizabeth went up to her and placed her hand on the girl's shoulder.

"God will bless you for what you have done," she said quietly. "You have given your children a chance to be happy and healthy." Mother Elizabeth slipped a small icon into Pelagia's hand. "Pray to the Mother of God whenever you can. She loves you and can give you the strength to break away from a sinful life." Pelagia clung to the icon and nodded while continuing to cry quietly. Mother Elizabeth slipped away. She knew that despite Pelagia's harsh words, she wanted to help her children. Helping Katya and Tanya meant giving them away to someone who could really care for them.

The nuns quickly gave out the rest of the food and medicine to other needy people in the slum. They then bundled Katya and Tanya into their carriage and drove back to the convent. Mother Elizabeth and Sister Barbara climbed out of the carriage and helped the children descend. The little girls looked around them in wonder at the beautiful garden that grew in front of the convent.

Small groves of birch trees waved in the breeze and neat gravel paths wound between colorful flowerbeds. The nuns led the children up to one of the white convent buildings and knocked on the door. A plump, cheerful-looking sister with round glasses opened the door.

"Good morning, mother!" she exclaimed while receiving the abbess's blessing.

"Hello, Sister Helen," said Mother Elizabeth. Little Katya and Tanya hid behind Sister Barbara, shaking. "We have two new charges for you today. Katya and Tanya—can you come out and greet Sister Helen?" The two children began to cry from fear and burrowed into Sister Barbara's habit.

"I have an idea," said Sister Helen quickly. She turned away from the door and called inside, "Zhenya! Please come here and bring Snowball." In a minute, a girl of about seven came to the door. She was neatly dressed in a long dress and apron, her head covered by a kerchief. She carried a large, fluffy white cat, who purred loudly as she stroked him. Zhenya went over to the children and knelt down next to them.

"Hello, children!" she said softly. "You don't have to be afraid. Everyone is very kind here. I too came from Khitrovka and I was frightened at first. Now I love it! Come, why don't you help me feed Snowball? It's time for his meal!"

As Zhenya talked, Katya and Tanya slowly stopped sobbing. Tanya tentatively reached out a hand to Snowball and began to pet him. He purred even louder and Katya let out a small giggle. Zhenya placed Snowball on the ground and took the little girls' hands and led them into the orphanage dormitory on the right. It was a bright, cheerful room decorated with framed prints of Russian fairy tales and lush green plants. A large icon of the Theotokos hung in the corner.

"Please take them to the hospital later to have Dr. Kornilov check them," said Mother Elizabeth in a low voice to Sister Helen. "They have many bruises, and I suspect that Tanya's leg may never have healed properly from a break. She limps quite a bit."

"Of course, mother," answered Sister Helen. "Don't you fear. We'll have them fattened up and smiling in no time!"

Mother Elizabeth and Sister Barbara walked back to the main building of the convent. Mother Elizabeth prayed silently, "Lord, thank you for guiding us to Tanya and Katya today. Watch over them and help them to heal from their wounds. Lord, also have mercy on their mother, Pelagia, and deliver her from the dark pit into which she has fallen."

"Well," she said, turning to Sister Barbara, "now we must begin our work for the day!"

Chapter Seven

Two years later, in 1915, life had become dangerous not only in Khitrovka but in all Moscow. In 1914, Russia had entered World War I. At first, the Russians were sure that the war would be short, but it soon became clear that this would not be so. Many Russian soldiers were killed as they fought against the Germans. As food was sent to the army, it became hard for ordinary people in Moscow to find certain items. Butter and eggs were almost impossible to buy, and even bread was in short supply. People waited in long lines outside bakeries hoping to buy a loaf or two. The Convent of Mary and Martha tried to bring vegetables and fruits from Mother Elizabeth's former estate at Ilinskoye. The carts carrying the food to the hospital patients and orphans at the convent were sometimes raided by people desperate for something to eat.

Not only were the ordinary people in Moscow hungry, they were also angry. Many were upset with Tsar Nicholas, Empress Alexandra, and the whole imperial government. They felt that the war was being badly managed. They also were very upset by the imperial couple's friendship with a man called Rasputin. Rasputin was a monk who Alexandra felt greatly helped her son Alexei. Alexei was ill with hemophilia* and was often in great pain from his disease. Alexandra felt that Rasputin's prayers helped to relieve her son.

What Alexandra did not know was that Rasputin did not always behave like a good person. Sometimes he held wild parties and made friends with immoral people. Many Russians knew about Rasputin's bad behavior and were scandalized that Nicholas and Alexandra continued to be friends with him. They did not understand that when Rasputin was with the royal couple, he acted very pious and kind. Many people in Moscow began to complain about Nicholas and Alexandra. They even referred to Alexandra as "the German woman" because she was born in Germany. Since Mother Elizabeth was Alexandra's sister, they began to accuse her also of being a traitor to Russia.

In April, 1915, a mob of Muscovites began to rage through the streets. They were very angry about a battle the Russian soldiers had lost to the German Army. The mob burned down many shops and factories owned by

---

* Hemophilia is a disorder in which a person's blood fails to clot properly. Consequently, even a slight cut or bruise can bleed profusely and cause a great deal of pain.

Germans. People in the crowd even shouted that Empress Alexandra was a German traitor and should be put in prison. They then decided to go attack Mother Elizabeth's convent because she was of German heritage too. No one seemed to remember all the kind things she had done for the people of Moscow over the last ten years.

Inside the Convent of Mary and Martha, the sisters were nervous. They tried to perform their usual duties, but outside they could hear shouting and windows breaking. The loud, drunken voices seemed to be getting very close to the convent. Mother Elizabeth was working in the hospital, helping to bandage a burn on a woman's leg.

"Mother," a soft voice said next to her.

"Yes, Sister Barbara?" asked Mother Elizabeth calmly.

"We are all frightened. The crowd has just attacked a German piano store a few blocks from here! They may come here next!"

"I will talk to them," said Mother Elizabeth firmly. "They are drunk and don't know what they're doing."

Just as she said this, a stone smashed through one of the hospital windows, narrowly missing one of the nuns. Several patients began to cry from fear.

"Sisters!" Mother Elizabeth called out. "Move the beds to the far end of the room!"

The nuns working in the hospital quickly began to wheel the hospital beds away from the windows. Another large stone broke a pane of glass and clanged against an operating table. From below, the sisters heard men shouting, "Give us the accursed German!"

"I am going out to talk to them," Mother Elizabeth said quietly to Sister Barbara. "If anything happens, you are in charge."

"No, Mother, please!" urged Sister Barbara anxiously. "It's much too dangerous!"

Mother Elizabeth left the hospital and walked toward the convent's main door. After taking a deep breath and saying a quiet prayer, she opened the heavy door as several nuns cowered in the background. A crowd of about thirty drunken men stood shouting and cursing in front of the convent. Several were taking deep swigs from vodka bottles. "There's the traitor!" one shouted. "Go back to Germany where you belong!" yelled another. Others seemed shocked, though, to see Mother Elizabeth dressed in a simple gray habit. "Is that really the empress's sister?" they muttered.

"Please, gentlemen," said Mother Elizabeth in a loud voice, "I must ask you to leave our convent. Your shouts are disturbing our hospital patients. We have many ill people we are trying to help!"

At her words, some of the men seemed confused and a bit ashamed. They slowly began to drift away. A few others, though, began to get even angrier. Shouting, "Get rid of the German!" they surged toward Mother Elizabeth. Just in time, Sister Agatha managed to pull Mother Elizabeth back into the convent and close the door. As she locked it with shaking hands, a hail of rocks hit the building and smashed several more windows. Terrified, the sisters looked at each other, not knowing what to do. Just then, they heard the welcome sound of horses' hooves. A troop of soldiers galloped up to the convent and began to fight back the mob. The nuns heard loud screams as the soldiers smashed at the crowd with nightsticks.

After about an hour, the shouts outside quieted and a knock was heard at the convent door. One of the nuns

cautiously opened it. Outside
stood a sweating soldier, holding his helmet. He made a
short bow to the sister.

"You sisters don't have to
worry now," he told her, "we
took care of those scum.
Most of them ran away,
and the rest won't be
doing any harm for a
while." He chortled
and pointed at some

bloody and groaning men lying next to the building.

"Thank you, young man," said the sister in a weak
voice as he and the other soldiers galloped off. Mother
Elizabeth stepped forward.

"Quickly, sisters," she said, "help me to bring the injured people up to the hospital!"

The nuns struggled together to carry the wounded
attackers inside.

One of the men, still conscious but bleeding from a
gash in the head, looked wonderingly up at Mother Elizabeth and asked in a faint voice, "Why are you helping us?
We tried to kill you and smash up the convent."

"Right now you are simply an injured man and, like
the Samaritan, I am called on by the Lord to help you,"
said Mother Elizabeth simply. "Now don't talk. It will
only weaken you."

Things continued to get worse in Russia. In March of
1917, a large crowd of people in St. Petersburg who had
waited all night outside a bakery hoping to buy bread
became desperate from hunger. Bolshevik (Communist)

leaders who wanted to overthrow the tsar gave the people red banners that read "Bread and Peace." Urged on by the Bolshevik leaders, the angry crowd marched through the city, shouting for the war to end. On March 9, troops were ordered to fire on the protesters, and many marchers were killed. But only two days later, when another regiment was told to fire on another group of protesters, the soldiers refused. They even began to kill their own officers. When a huge crowd of revolutionary marchers stormed down Nevsky Prospect, St. Petersburg's main street, another regiment of soldiers lifted their guns and rushed in to join the mob. On March 15, Tsar Nicholas II at last realized that he no longer had control in his country and consented to give up his throne. A new "provisional" government including communists, socialists, and parliamentary democrats was formed.

The nuns at the Saints Mary and Martha Convent were frightened of the huge changes taking place in Russia. They did not know what would happen to them now that a new government was in power. The nuns held prayer vigils day and night and hoped that God would protect them and their country. One day a group of drunken Bolshevik soldiers came to arrest Mother Elizabeth during a church service, but became ashamed when they heard the prayers being sung by the nuns. They left without taking her. Later in the month, the mayor of Moscow offered to take Mother Elizabeth into the Kremlin building for protection. Mother Elizabeth refused to leave the convent sisters alone.

In April, as she sat drinking tea and writing some letters in her cell, Mother Elizabeth heard a quiet knock at her door.

"Come in!" she called out.

Sister Barbara peeked in. "Mother," she said softly, "there is an important visitor here to see you. The Swedish Ambassador."

Mother Elizabeth was puzzled but said, "Send him in, please."

A distinguished but nervous-looking man entered the room. "Are you the Abbess Elizabeth?" he asked, his eyes darting around the room. He seemed to expect a frightening revolutionary to leap at him from behind the curtains or from under the bed.

"Yes, I am," answered Mother Elizabeth. "What can I do for you?"

The ambassador sat down on a simple wooden chair near the abbess's door. In a low voice he said, "I have a letter for you, abbess. It has come from Germany. It was sent to me after much difficulty and I have promised to pass it to you personally. It may save your life."

The man carefully handed Mother Elizabeth a simple white envelope, which she quickly opened. Inside was a letter from Kaiser Wilhelm, the emperor of Germany. This was the same William who had long ago proposed marriage to young Ella. The letter stated that the emperor was frightened for her safety and promised her an escort back to Germany and a permanent home when she got there.

Mother Elizabeth read the letter carefully and felt touched. Who would have thought that Wilhelm would still feel concern for her after all these years? It was especially moving since Mother Elizabeth was the sister-in-law of Tsar Nicholas, the man who had been leading Russia in the war against Germany. Mother Elizabeth sat quietly for a minute and then turned to the ambassador.

"Please convey to his highness that I am very touched by his kind offer, but that I must refuse. I cannot abandon my convent at this time. I am responsible for the sisters here, and as the situation worsens here in Russia, more people will need to use our hospital, pharmacy, and cafeteria. Russia has become my true country, and I cannot leave her."

The ambassador looked shocked and upset. "But my dear abbess!" he exclaimed. "Perhaps you do not realize that the Bolshevik leader Lenin has left Germany and will be arriving soon in Russia. He is a bloodthirsty and ambitious man who will try to seize power at any cost. You are not safe in Moscow!"

"I realize that," answered Mother Elizabeth calmly. "However, I am in God's hands. If He wishes to deliver me from these enemies, He will do so. If not, I will be honored to win a martyr's crown." With that she firmly thanked the ambassador again and asked him to leave. Shaking his head in disbelief, the man exited the convent.

Mother Elizabeth walked over to her icon corner and began to pray once again for the deliverance of Russia from its enemies: "Through the intercessions of Thy most pure Mother, save the suffering Russian people from the yoke of godless authority. . ." As she finished her prayers, Mother Elizabeth looked over at the bookcase next to her. On one shelf stood a photograph of herself and her sisters and brother, taken many years before in Hesse. Sadly, she realized that she might never see any of them again.

Chapter Eight

Almost a year later, in April of 1918, Mother Elizabeth stood in the convent chapel with the other sisters. It was Bright Week, the week following Easter, and the nuns were in a cheerful mood. The air inside was chilly due to the city's fuel shortage, but the sisters felt warm because of just having celebrated the Feast of the Resurrection. As Vespers ended and the nuns began to file out of the chapel, a loud bang sounded through the building. Then several more followed. The nuns looked at each other nervously.

"It's the door, Mother," Sister Catherine stated fearfully. "Shall I answer it?"

"Yes, go ahead," said Mother Elizabeth. "I'll follow you in a minute."

Mother Elizabeth knew that having visitors who knocked angrily on the convent door at night was not a good sign. Life in Moscow had become lawless and dangerous. The Bolsheviks had invaded Moscow the previous October and had taken over leadership of Russia. Since then, constant fighting went on in the streets. Criminals had been let out of prison; they stole and attacked people without being punished. On the other hand, anyone who disagreed with the Bolshevik ideas was arrested and imprisoned in a huge fortress called the Lubianka. Some fifty thousand were shot. The imperial family were taken by guards to the town of Tobolsk. Food was scarce, and the convent sisters ate very little so that enough would be left for the patients in their hospital.

With shaking hands, Sister Catherine opened the convent doors. Outside stood a large group of Bolshevik officers. A tall, grim-faced man stepped forward.

"We have come for the Abbess Elizabeth. Allow me to enter," he ordered in a harsh voice.

"I am Abbess Elizabeth," said Mother Elizabeth, stepping forward. Behind her some of the younger nuns began to cry softly.

"Elizabeth Fyodorovna," the soldier said, disrespectfully addressing Mother Elizabeth by her secular name, "we have orders to take you away from Moscow for your safety."

"I understand," said Mother Elizabeth calmly. "May I have two hours to say goodbye to the sisters and to gather my things?"

"You may have half an hour. That should be plenty of time," the soldier replied rudely.

Mother Elizabeth quickly went to her room and placed

a few possessions into a small, worn suitcase. She then gathered the sisters and said goodbye to each one personally, thanking them for their love and hard work. She also thanked Father Mitrophan, the convent priest, and asked him to say a short prayer service. Two nuns, Sister Barbara and Sister Catherine, begged to be allowed to leave with Mother Elizabeth, and the Bolshevik soldiers consented. Trying not to cry, Mother Elizabeth waved goodbye a final time to the convent sisters and climbed into the car outside.

Mother Elizabeth, Sister Barbara, and Sister Catherine were taken to a nearby train station, where they were forced to board a guarded carriage. They were herded into a compartment at the back. The train looked nothing like the clean, pleasant machines that Mother Elizabeth remembered from peaceful times. The seats were torn and dirty and the floors covered with mud. Many windows were broken, and a cold wind blew through the nuns' compartment. The nuns were alone, but they could see that the train's other carriages were crammed full. People were pushing and shoving their way on, and many were climbing onto the roofs out of desperation. The train started to move with a loud screeching noise. Soon it was rolling through the countryside on its way to Siberia.

"Mother," said Sister Catherine suddenly, after an hour or so had gone by, "look outside!"

Mother Elizabeth and Sister Barbara peered out through the scratched windows. "Those are bodies!" Sister Barbara exclaimed in horror. Every few minutes, the train passed another body lying near the train tracks. It was apparent that many people had fallen off the train roofs and been killed.

Two days later their train at last sputtered to a stop in the Siberian city of Yekaterinburg. The nuns could see red banners flying everywhere and felt at once that they were in the heart of enemy territory. Soon a young guard entered their compartment and ordered them off the train. They were hustled into a waiting cart and driven to the Novotikhvinsky Convent outside the city. The convent was being used as a prison, and as she was shoved into her prison cell, Mother Elizabeth could see other members of the imperial family being taken in by guards.

A few weeks later, Mother Elizabeth, Sister Catherine, and Sister Barbara were moved again. This time they were taken to the town of Alapayevsk, about one hundred miles north of Yekaterinburg. It was a warm May morning when the wagon in which the nuns were riding at last pulled up in front of the Alapayevsk elementary school. The nuns' legs were sore and stiff from the long ride over rough dirt roads. Their driver hopped off the wagon.

"Well, here's your new home. Not exactly a palace, is it?" he laughed nastily.

The school was small and built of faded brick. A broken shutter flapped at one of the windows. The yard in front was full of dandelions and other scraggly weeds.

Mother Elizabeth tried not to be depressed at the thought of living in such a ramshackle place.

"Well," she said, turning to Sister Barbara, "if they let us, I think we might be able to plant a kitchen garden here. I'm dying for some fresh vegetables!"

As it turned out, the nuns *were* allowed to plant a garden. They were also given other small privileges. To Mother Elizabeth's joy, she was able to attend church at a nearby monastery. Father Seraphim, one of the monks, became her confessor. On pleasant days, the nuns took long walks in the fields outside town. The soldiers who guarded them trusted that the women would not try to escape. Nearly every afternoon, Mother Elizabeth and the sisters would drink tea and chat out in the schoolyard.

"Our tomatoes will soon be ripe," commented Sister Barbara.

"That's thanks to your green thumb," said Mother Elizabeth, smiling. "I could never coax anything to grow in this soil."

"Well," said Sister Barbara modestly, "it comes from having gardening in the blood. My mother grew vegetables to make your mouth water! And such apples too!"

The nuns tried to stay cheerful even though they had no idea what might happen to them in the future. Realistically, they knew that the Bolsheviks might decide to execute them at any moment. Mother Elizabeth prayed constantly that she be granted the courage to face her fate, whatever it might be. When the sisters became frightened or gloomy, the abbess did her best to lift their spirits.

Slowly the guards in charge of the nuns became more strict. The prisoners could no longer go to church or take walks in the fields. All of their possessions except the clothes and shoes they wore were taken away. Toward the middle of the summer, Mother Elizabeth and the sisters were forced to stay in their rooms all day. The heat was terrible, and the nuns could not open the locked windows in order to cool the house.

The nuns were never given news of what was happening in the outside world. They had no newspapers and could not talk to outsiders. They did not know that people who disagreed with the Bolsheviks' communist ideas had organized a White Army to fight Lenin and the Reds. The White Army was winning battles and coming close to invading Yekaterinburg. The Bolsheviks were afraid to lose power, so they decided to commit a terrible act. The former Tsar Nicholas, Alexandra, and their children had been imprisoned in the city. On July 17, 1918, the imperial family was told to climb down into the basement of the house where they were living. They were then read a death sentence and shot by a group of Bolshevik soldiers.

The next day, a group of Bolshevik guards entered the schoolhouse where Mother Elizabeth and the others were imprisoned. Mother Elizabeth had been praying in her room, and as she heard the rude voices shouting in the hall, she knew that the end was near. Startsev, the policeman in charge of the men, barged into Mother Elizabeth's room.

"Get up!" he ordered the abbess. "I am here to tell you that in a few hours you will be taken to a mineshaft north of this town. Long live the revolution!" Startsev didn't add that the prisoners would be executed there, but he did not need to say so. Everyone understood that their life on earth was almost over.

After a small meal, Mother Elizabeth, Sister Barbara, and a few other royal prisoners who had been living in the school were shoved roughly into wooden carts. Mother Elizabeth and Sister Barbara sat together. Sister Barbara began to weep quietly.

"Mother," she said in a quivering voice, "I want to have courage, but all I feel is fear. My sins are so many . . . we have not had confession for weeks. I am not prepared to die!"

"Sister," said Mother Elizabeth reassuringly, "our Lord understands that we are not able to receive the last sacraments. He will forgive! We must be strong for the others here and set a good example so that they may die in peace." With those words, she began to sing "O Gladsome Light," a beautiful hymn from the Orthodox Vespers service. Sister Barbara joined in, though her voice cracked often. Other voices from the carts behind them began to sing also.

"Get out, all of you!" ordered one of the soldiers as they stopped in a small grove. "Walk in that direction!" he added, pointing his bayonet into the gloom.

The prisoners walked slowly toward a dark chasm that yawned in front of them. An eerie creaking noise came from the abandoned mineshaft.

"Stop!" yelled out Startsev as the prisoners came near to the shaft's opening. "You enemies of the Russian people have been sentenced to death. At last justice will prevail!"

With these words, he pulled Mother Elizabeth forward roughly. She knelt down by the edge of the pit.

"May I pray for a moment?" the abbess asked softly.

"Make it quick!" Startsev answered harshly.

"Father, forgive them, for they know not what they do!" Mother Elizabeth prayed and crossed herself. At that moment a soldier struck her on the head with a rifle butt. Several other soldiers threw her still-breathing body down into the sixty-foot mineshaft.

The other prisoners were either shot or bludgeoned and thrown into the pit after the abbess. The soldiers next threw planks of wood and loose rock down on top of them. Finally, Startsev tossed a lighted grenade into the mineshaft. The soldiers ran from the pit's opening as a loud explosion ripped through the air.

Early the next morning, Father Seraphim, Mother

Elizabeth's confessor from the monastery, crept fearfully into the forest. Another monk had seen the carts the evening before and had told Father Seraphim that he thought something terrible had happened to the prisoners. Father Seraphim walked toward the abandoned mineshaft. As he approached the opening, his disbelieving ears heard weak voices singing church hymns. Sadly, over the next few hours, each voice grew silent. Weeping, Father Seraphim realized that Mother Elizabeth and the others had died. Kneeling by the pit, the monk began to pray, "Into Thy hands, O Lord, I commend the souls of Thy servants, and ask Thee to grant them rest . . . for Thou art the Resurrection, and the Life, and the repose of Thy departed servants . . ."

Emulating the Lord's self-abasement on the earth,
You gave up royal mansions to serve the poor and disdained,
Overflowing with compassion for the suffering.
And taking up a martyr's cross,
In your meekness
You perfected the Saviour's image within yourself,
Therefore, with Barbara, entreat
Him to save us all, O wise Elizabeth.
—*Troparion in tone 4*

Afterword

In September of 1918, the White Army invaded Alapayevsk, and the Bolsheviks fled. Father Seraphim brought the White Army leaders to the abandoned mineshaft. Soldiers began to dig out the debris that covered the bodies of Mother Elizabeth and those who died with her. When they reached the bottom of the pit, Father Seraphim and the others were astonished at what they saw. Mother Elizabeth's body was found lying next to that of another victim. The abbess's veil had been torn apart and used to bandage the young man's wounds. Even as she lay dying, Mother Elizabeth had cared for others.

Mother Elizabeth's body, together with the others, was raised to the surface. With great courage, Father Seraphim then transported the abbess's remains across Russia by train. The Civil War was raging in the country, and many times the monk's life was in danger. In 1920, Father Seraphim at last reached China, where Mother Elizabeth's coffin was placed in an Orthodox church in Beijing. A few months later, the abbess's dream of being buried in Jerusalem was realized when her body was brought to the Church of St. Mary Magdalene. This was the same church whose consecration Mother Elizabeth had witnessed many years before. The abbess's remains were kept in the church and watched over by Father Seraphim.

In 1982, the Orthodox Church formally recognized Mother Elizabeth's sainthood. She, Sister Barbara, and many other martyrs of the Russian Communists were canonized by the Church. Today, pilgrims can venerate Saint Elizabeth the New Martyr at the Church of St. Mary Magdalene in Jerusalem.

Bibliography

Mager, Hugo. *Elizabeth, Grand Duchess of Russia*. New York: Carrol & Graf. 1998.

The Martha-Mary Convent and Rule of St. Elizabeth the New Martyr. Jordanville, New York: Printshop of St. Job of Pochaev. 1991.